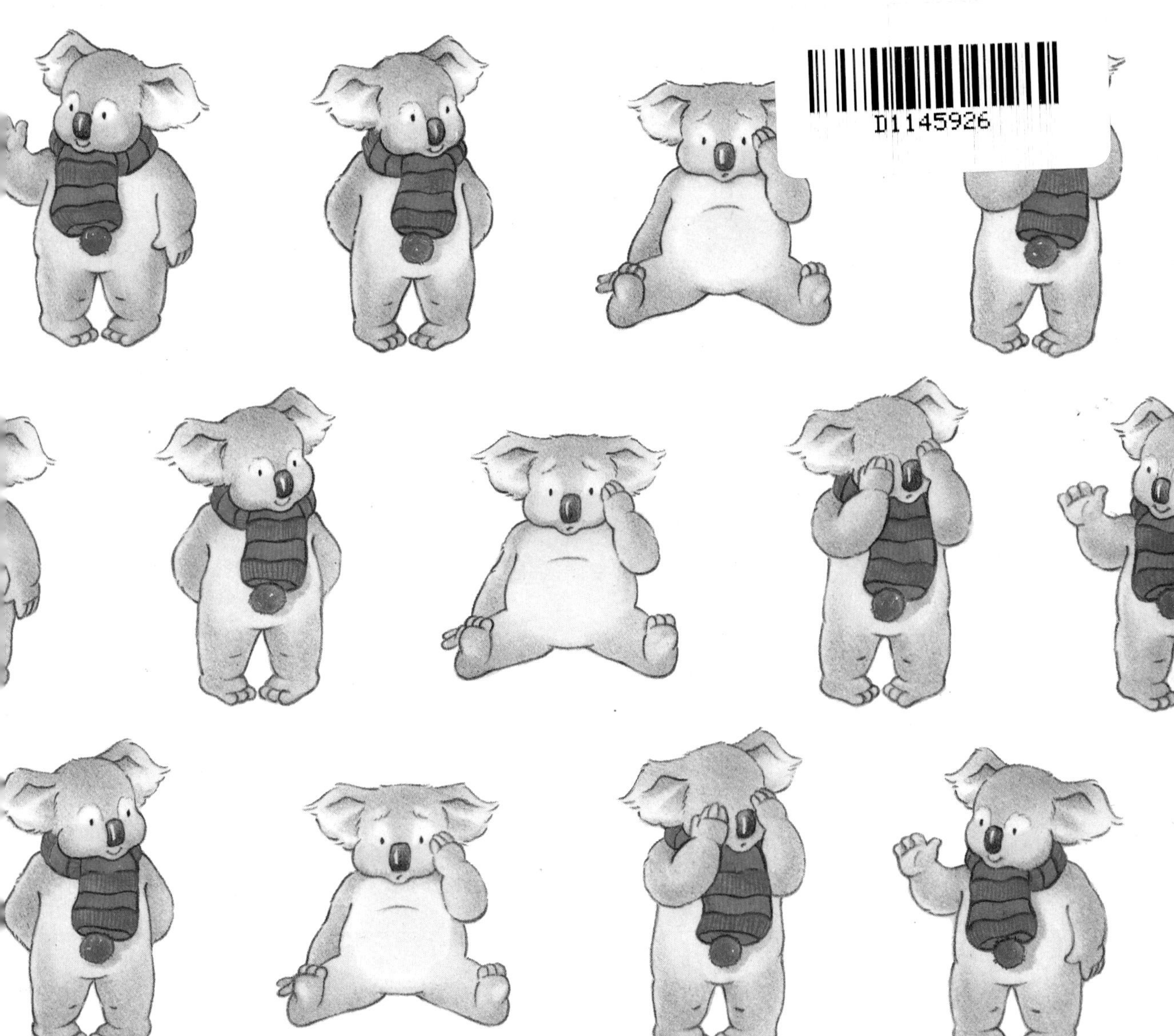

D1145926

British Library Cataloguing in Publication Data

Stimson, Joan
Kim meets Santa Claus.
I. Title II. Matthews, Anne, *1960-*
823.914 [J]

ISBN 0-7214-9615-6

First edition

Published by Ladybird Books Ltd Loughborough Leicestershire UK
Ladybird Books Inc Auburn Maine 04210 USA

© LADYBIRD BOOKS LTD MCMXC
All rights reserved. No part of this publication may be reproduced, stored in a retrieval system, or transmitted in any form or by any means, electronic, mechanical, photo-copying, recording or otherwise, without the prior consent of the copyright owner.

Printed in England (3)

Kim meets Santa Claus

written by JOAN STIMSON
illustrated by ANNE MATTHEWS

Ladybird

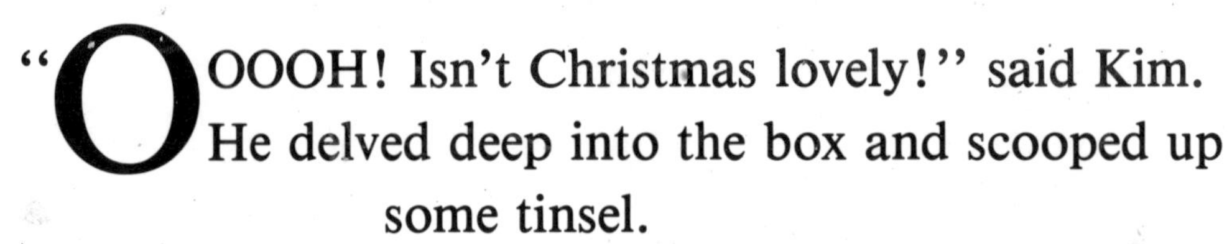

"OOOOH! Isn't Christmas lovely!" said Kim. He delved deep into the box and scooped up some tinsel.

"Watch out!" cried Peter. "It's meant to go on the tree... not round your ears."

Peter sorted through the decorations. "Reindeer, baubles, snowflakes, snowmen, bell..."

"Oh no!" cried Kim suddenly.
He sat down by the tree in a heap.

"What's the matter?"
asked Peter.

"It's my letter to Santa
Claus," replied Kim.
"I've just remembered...
I forgot."

“Forgot what?” said Peter.

“I forgot to ask for my SPECIAL PRESENT.”

“Oh Kim!” cried Peter. “It’s much too late to send another letter. How ever did you forget? And what IS your SPECIAL PRESENT anyway?”

Kim drew himself up. "It's private," he said. "And I was thinking how to spell other things."

"But JAM's easy to spell," said Peter, knowing it was Kim's favourite.

"STRAWBERRY's not," said Kim in a small voice. "It took ages."

Kim stared gloomily into space while Peter finished the tree.

Then, just as he was fixing the star on top, Peter had a brainwave.

"Kim," he said, "Santa Claus is in town today. There was a notice in my comic. We can find him at the department store, and tell him about your SPECIAL PRESENT."

Kim cheered up immediately at this suggestion. He scuttled round and round in small circles.

The two friends got ready for the bus. Kim made some sandwiches with the last of his jam.

"For Santa Claus," he explained. "It's a long way back to the North Pole."

By the time the bus came Kim was squeaking with excitement.

"Two tickets to Santa Claus," he told the driver.

By the time the bus reached town, the SEAT was squeaking, because Kim couldn't sit still.

Kim and Peter stood in front of the notice.

They ran up the stairs together and took their place in the queue.

"I want the biggest doll in the whole world," cried a cross girl. "What do YOU want?" she asked Kim.

"Ahem! It's a private, sharey sort of present," said Kim politely.

"Huh!" said the cross girl. "I won't share anything I get."

As the children chattered in the queue Kim grew more and more impatient.

TOY
DEPARTMENT

"Imagine ME!" cried Kim every few minutes. "Imagine ME... seeing Santa Claus!"

At last the cross girl went in. And came out again, even crosser.

"That's not fair!" she cried. "He wouldn't promise anything. I might not get the biggest doll after all. I HATE Santa Claus!"

All of a sudden Kim was nervous.

"Oh Peter," he whispered. "What if Santa Claus is cross with ME? What if he doesn't like people asking for MORE?"

“NEXT!” boomed a voice from behind the curtain. Peter gave Kim a shove. And there he was… face to face with Santa Claus.

Kim looked up at the big boots and the big beard.

“Please, sir,” whispered Kim. “I want to go home.”

Santa Claus smiled. He spoke in a soft, kind voice. “Of course,” he said. “But perhaps we can have a little chat first?”

Kim began to feel a little less nervous. He unwrapped his sandwiches.

"You can eat them now or on your way back to the North Pole," he explained.

"How thoughtful!" said Santa Claus. "It's not often someone brings ME a present. Perhaps we should BOTH have one."

Kim felt better after his sandwich. He started to tell Santa Claus all about his friend Peter. And how they'd written their Christmas letters together.

"And then I was so busy thinking how to spell STRAWBERRY that I forgot to write down my SPECIAL PRESENT."

"And what would that be?" asked Santa Claus.

All of a sudden Kim felt shy again. Santa Claus bent down and Kim stood on tiptoe... to whisper in his ear.

Santa Claus smiled.

"Rather a lot of children have asked for that already," he said. "And some grown-ups. In my job," he went on, "I can't promise to do EVERYTHING. I can only promise to do MY BEST."

"Oh thank you," said Kim. "Thank you, Santa Claus. And have a safe journey back to the North Pole."

Kim scuttled out to find Peter.

"He's going to do HIS BEST," he whispered, as they left the shop.

Picture books

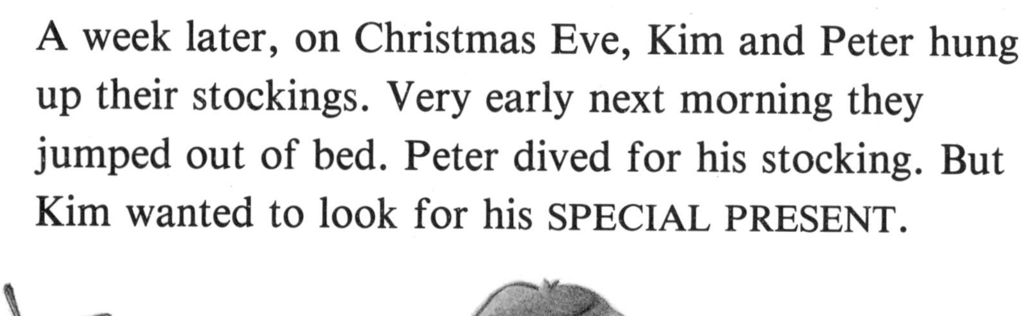

A week later, on Christmas Eve, Kim and Peter hung up their stockings. Very early next morning they jumped out of bed. Peter dived for his stocking. But Kim wanted to look for his SPECIAL PRESENT.

"I do hope it's come,"
he whispered. Gently he pulled back the curtains.

"OOOOH! It HAS come. Santa Claus DID do HIS BEST. Isn't Christmas lovely," whispered Kim, "...especially WHEN IT SNOWS!"

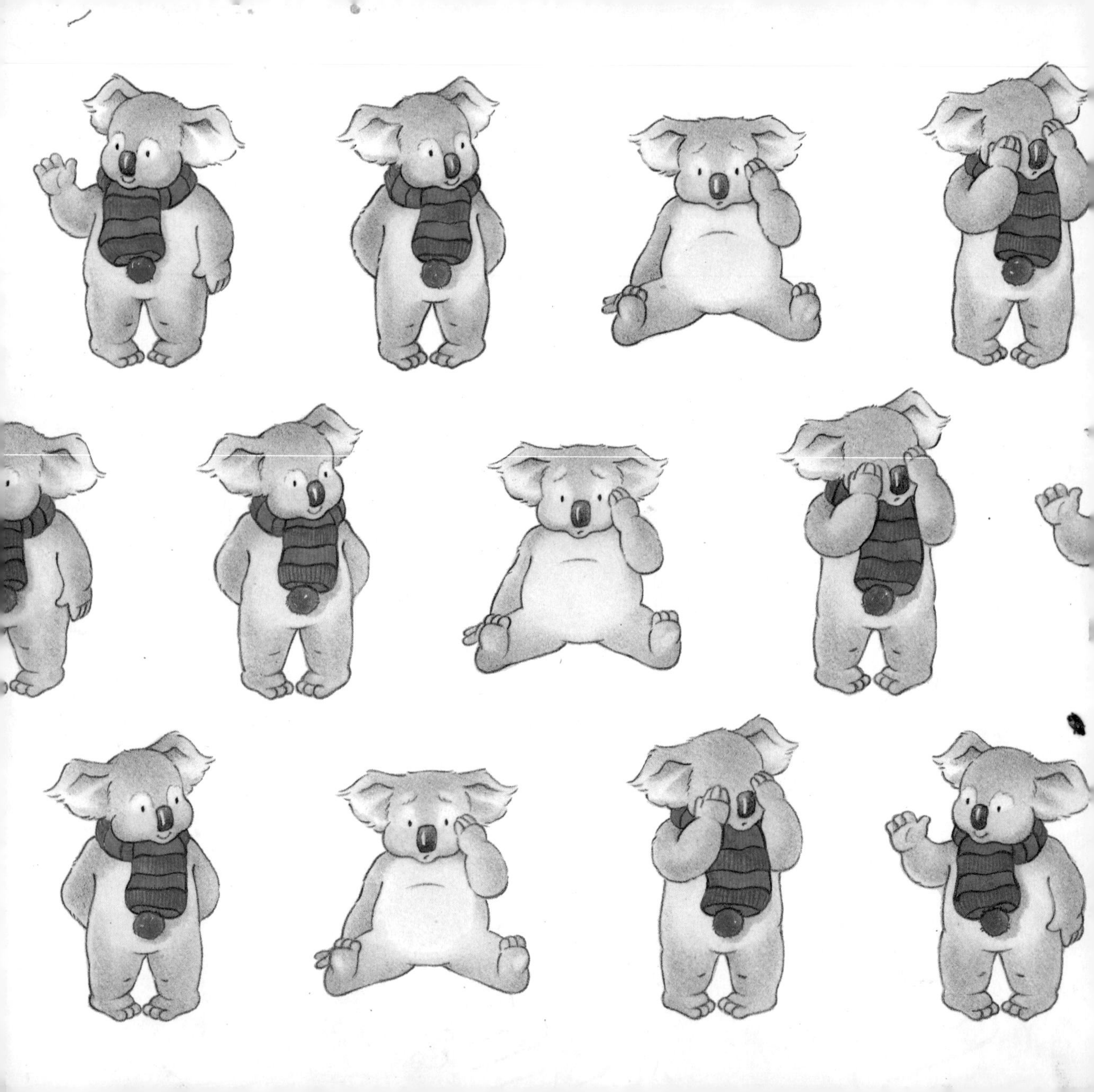